SkippyjonJones

IN
MUMMY
TROUBLE

JUDY SCHACHNER

PUFFIN BOOKS

For Carol and Steve and muchas gracias *to:*
Lucia, Stephanie, Heather, Sara R., Sarah P.,
and the many who make Skippy bounce.

Con mucho cariño,
Mamalita

PUFFIN BOOKS
Published by the Penguin Group
Penguin Young Readers Group, 345 Hudson Street, New York, New York 10014, U.S.A.
Penguin Group (Canada), 90 Eglinton Avenue East, Suite 700, Toronto, Ontario,
Canada M4P 2Y3 (a division of Pearson Penguin Canada Inc.)
Penguin Books Ltd, 80 Strand, London WC2R 0RL, England
Penguin Ireland, 25 St Stephen's Green, Dublin 2, Ireland
(a division of Penguin Books Ltd)
Penguin Group (Australia), 250 Camberwell Road, Camberwell, Victoria 3124, Australia
(a division of Pearson Australia Group Pty Ltd)
Penguin Books India Pvt Ltd, 11 Community Centre, Panchsheel Park, New Delhi - 110 017, India
Penguin Group (NZ), 67 Apollo Drive, Rosedale, North Shore 0632, New Zealand
(a division of Pearson New Zealand Ltd)
Penguin Books (South Africa) (Pty) Ltd, 24 Sturdee Avenue,
Rosebank, Johannesburg 2196, South Africa

Registered Offices: Penguin Books Ltd, 80 Strand, London WC2R 0RL, England

First published in the United States of America by Dutton Children's Books,
a division of Penguin Young Readers Group, 2006
Published by Puffin Books, a division of Penguin Young Readers Group, 2008

1 2 3 4 5 6 7 8 9 10

Copyright © Judith Byron Schachner, 2006
All rights reserved

THE LIBRARY OF CONGRESS HAS CATALOGED THE DUTTON CHILDREN'S BOOKS EDITION AS FOLLOWS:
Schachner, Judith Byron.
Skippyjon Jones in mummy trouble / Judy Schachner.—1st ed.
p. cm.
Summary: Skippyjon Jones, a Siamese kitten who thinks he's a Chihuahua, dreams of traveling
to ancient Egypt with his gang of Chihuahua *amigos.*
ISBN: 0-525-47754-3 (hc)
[1. Siamese cat—Fiction. 2. Cats—Fiction. 3. Chihuahua (Dog breed)—Fiction. 4. Dogs—Fiction.
5. Mummies—Fiction.] I. Title.
PZ7.S3286Sjm 2006 [E]—dc22 2006000934

Puffin Books ISBN 978-0-14-241211-4

Designed by Heather Wood
Manufactured in China
The illustrations for this book were created in acrylics and pen and ink on Aquarelle Arches
watercolor paper.

Skippyjon Jones did his very best thinking outside the box.

And this twisted his mama's whiskers tighter than a Texas tornado.

"Hey, you, Mr. McPooh," said Mama Junebug Jones, "just what do you think you're doing?"

NATIONAL LEOGRAPHIC
CAT MUMMIES

McPooh didn't say boo.
He was too busy reading.

"Hey, Little Digger—I'm talking to you," said Mama, scooping up her boy. "A pyramid outside the litter box will never ever do."

Then she saw his magazine.

"*National Leographic!*" mused Mama. "And 'The Curse of the Cat-mummy.'

"Why, this will give you

nightmares, boy,

with an **upset**

tummy, too.

Plus a **puffy** tail

on the

grandest

scale.

This story is ***taboo!***"

But Skippyjon Jones was in no mood to listen to his mama, so he skedaddled into his room . . .

He **bounced** once,

he **bounced** twice,

. . . for a really good bounce on
his big-boy bed.

and the third time he

BOUNCED

he said:

"Oh, I'm *Skippyjonjones*,
And I do love my mummy.
But if I don't bounce,
I get knots in my tummy!"

Then the kitty boy flipped over to the mirror for a look-see.

"HOLY SMOKE-ito!" exclaimed Skippyjon Jones. "I know you!" he said to the doggie in the mirror.

"Your ears are too big for your head. Your head is too big for your body. You are not a *Siamese cat!*"

Then, using his very best Spanish accent, he added, "You are steel the beeg **Chihuahua**, dude, the whole **Enchilada!**"

And they just might like enchiladas in Egypt, thought Skippy. So the kitty boy donned his mask and cape and began to sing in a *muy* soft voice.

"My name is Skippito Friskito, (clap-clap)

And I'm off to see old Egypt-ito. (clap-clap)

My chicos insist,

And I dare not resist

The chance to go meet a mummito." (clap-clap)

In the meantime, his little sisters, Jezebel, Jilly Boo, and
Ju-Ju Bee, rolled into his room with a plan of their own.

But the kitty boy was already deep inside
his closet on his way to ancient Egypt.

And paddling down the river Nile, who should sail right past but a kooky crocodile. Hunkered down on his lumpy, bumpy back were all his old *amigos*, the Chimichangos pack.

"*¿Adónde vas?*"
called out Skippito.

"We are going to the Under Mundo,"
answered the Chihuahuas.

"Not to the Underwear!"
exclaimed Skippito.

"No, no, no," said the poochitos. "You seely leetle beast!

To the **Under World**

where mummitos rest in **_peas_**."

"_Peas?_" exclaimed Skippito.
"Who wants to sleep in _peas_?"
"We do!" said the doggies.
"We hear they are to die for."

"You mean they are better than the *frijoles*?" asked Skippito.

"*Sí, mucho mejor, señor,*" said Poquito Tito.

"*¡Vámonos!*" said Skippito. "What are we waiting for?"

But then Don Diego, the biggest of the small ones, spoke up. "Hold your ponies, Pepito. To get to the Under Mundo, we first have to answer the Reedle of the Finx."

"But I'm not good at reedles,"
said Skippito.
"*No problema,*" said Poquito Tito.
"You have a *muy* big brain."

Then they set forth from the *rio* Nile
to find the Finx. The *muchachos* began
to sing:

"Skippee-Skippooh-Skippito!

We only have one chance-erito

To pass by the Finx,

So don't be a jinx.

Just answer the

Riddle-dum-dito!"

The *muchachos* arrived at four o'clock sharp. But the Finx had been waiting forever.

"Don't let the *gato* get your tongue, dude," said Don Diego.

"What cat, where?" asked Skippito.

"That cat there," said the *perritos*, pointing to the Finx.

But before he could say anything, the Great Finx spoke.

"Whose ears are too big for his **head?**

And who loves to go bounce on his **bed?**

Who creeps on all **fours,**

Through his own closet **door,**

Straight into the **Land of the Dead?**"

Skippito knew the answer to
this riddle, but he was so nervous
he coughed up a little fur ball.
    "You call that an answer, dude?"
said Don Diego.

"THE
Answer!"
bellowed the Finx.

So with his permission, the *perritos*
were free to pass on to the tomb of
King Rootin-Tootin-Kitten-Kabootin.

When they finally reached the pyramid, the doggies burst into song and dance.

O-si, o-say, Osiris, (clap-clap)
Our boy had a touch of the virus. (clap-clap)
He coughed up a ball,
So the Finx made a call,
And now it's inscribed on papyrus.
(clap-clap)

But when Skippito saw how dark it looked in the pyramid, he began to feel queasy.

"My tummy hurts," he groaned. "And my tail is getting puffy, too."

But his *chicos* would not comfort him. They just wanted their peas, *por favor*!

"Are you not El Skippito Friskito, the great sword fighter?" asked Poquito Tito.

"*Sí*," declared Skippito. "That is me."

"Then do your duty, dog," commanded Don Diego.

So Skippito drew in a deep breath and dove
into the darkness of the musty old tomb, chanting
peas por favor, peas por favor, peas por favor.

He rocketed through the vault
like a fur-covered comet.

Until suddenly, **Smack-ito!** Skippito hit a wall

Soon after, three goddesses emerged from the shadows to prepare the kitty boy for his journey to the Under Mundo.

"First we salt and pepper him," said Ba, the first goddess.

"And sprinkle him with lucky charms," said Da, the second one.

"Then we wrap him and roll him and bundle him tight," said Bing, the third goddess. "And blow him a kiss and say nighty-night."

Then the trio rolled the wrapped cat down the ramp into the king's burial chamber. Across the room stood the four-thousand-year-old sarcophagus of King Rootin-Tootin-Kitten-Kabootin.

And just as they were about to deliver El Skippito Mummito, he rolled right into the feet of the oldy, moldy mummy.

"Ba-Da-Bing," moaned the king as he stretched out his paws. "I need to rest in peace."

"Peas!" screamed El Skippito Mummito, waking up in a flash.

And quicker than you can say "mummies, mumps, and measles," he grabbed two pawsful of peas and hightailed it home.

When Los Chimichangos saw El Skippito Mummito come rolling out of the pyramid, they went into a real tailspin.

Then all the doggies began to chant:

"Green chícharos *hot,*

Green chícharos *cold,*

The best chícharos *in the world*

Are those that Skippito holds!"

But El Skippito Mummito was too scared to slow down, so he chucked the peas at his *chicos* and kept right on running . . .

. . . straight into the arms of his mummy.

"What's the matter, Fuzzy Bug?" asked Mama Junebug Jones.

Skippyjon Jones looked back over his shoulder to see if the three spirits were still chasing him.

"Ba-Da-Bing!" he wailed, dropping the last of the peas.

Then three giggling goddesses raced into the room after Skippito with their puppets and a roll of toilet paper.

"We're going to wrap you and roll you and bundle you tight!" they sang. "And check you for cooties, then kiss you good night."

That night Skippyjon Jones was bouncing on his big-boy bed.

"No mummies in my closet,
No mummies in my bed,
No mummies in my bookcase,
No mummies in my head."

Just before he closed his eyes, the kitty boy checked his room one more time for mummies. The only one he saw was his own.

"I love you, Mummy," said Skippyjon Jones.

"I love you, too, Bunny Boots," said Mama Junebug. "Now go to sleep, *por favor.*"